SEBASTIAN
(Super Sleuth)
and the Copycat Crime

Other books about Sebastian

Sebastian (Super Sleuth) and the
Baffling Bigfoot

Sebastian (Super Sleuth) and the
Bone to Pick Mystery

Sebastian (Super Sleuth) and the
Case of the Clumsy Cowboy

Sebastian (Super Sleuth) and the
Crummy Yummies Caper

Sebastian (Super Sleuth) and the
Egyptian Connection

Sebastian (Super Sleuth) and the
Impossible Crime

Sebastian (Super Sleuth) and the
Mystery Patient

Sebastian (Super Sleuth) and the
Purloined Sirloin

Sebastian (Super Sleuth) and the
Secret of the Skewered Skier

Sebastian (Super Sleuth) and the
Stars-in-His-Eyes Mystery

Sebastian (Super Sleuth) and the
Time Capsule Mystery

Mary Blount Christian

SEBASTIAN
(Super Sleuth)
and the Copycat Crime

Illustrated by Lisa McCue

MACMILLAN PUBLISHING COMPANY
New York

MAXWELL MACMILLAN CANADA
Toronto

MAXWELL MACMILLAN INTERNATIONAL
New York   Oxford   Singapore   Sydney

Macmillan Publishing Company is part of
the Maxwell Communication Group of Companies.

Macmillan Publishing Company
866 Third Avenue
New York, NY 10022

Maxwell Macmillan Canada, Inc.
1200 Eglinton Avenue East
Suite 200
Don Mills, Ontario M3C 3N1

First edition
Printed in the United States of America

10 9 8 7 6 5 4 3 2 1

The text of this book is set in 12 point Primer.
The illustrations are rendered in scratchboard.

Library of Congress Cataloging-in-Publication Data
Christian, Mary Blount.
Sebastian (Super Sleuth) and the copycat crime / Mary Blount
Christian ; illustrated by Lisa McCue. — 1st ed.
p.   cm.
Summary: While speaking at a crime writers' conference, bumbling
detective John Quincy Jones is aided by his capable canine in
solving the mystery of two missing manuscripts.
ISBN 0-02-718211-8
[1. Mystery and detective stories. 2. Dogs—Fiction.
3. Authors—Fiction.] I. McCue, Lisa, ill. II. Title.
PZ7.C4528Scu 1993   [Fic]—dc20   93-7038

For Vera Milz,
who brings children and books together

Contents

1
Running Out of Crime

Sebastian slowly uncurled himself on the couch and gave a long, lazy stretch and a satisfying yawn. *Mmmmmmmm.* A day off from crime solving.

It was John—John Quincy Jones—who was the official detective for the City Police Department, the one who got the paycheck. But it was he, Sebastian (Super Sleuth), who really solved the crimes, secretly leading his bungling partner through clue after clue to the solution.

The phone rang, and John answered it in his bedroom. With only the slightest of guilt pangs, Sebastian gently lifted the receiver of the extension phone and eavesdropped.

9

The voice on the line was raspy and hoarse, but it had the distinct grouchiness that identified the caller as Chief, John's boss.

"John, I've got a sore throat, so I want you to take my place today."

Sebastian's stub of a tail wriggled. Wow! He and John were going to be chief of police for a day!

"Sure, Chief!" John said. "I'll keep the old precinct—"

"Not as chief of police, you numskull," Chief croaked.

"Then replace you how and where, Chief?" John asked.

"At the crime-writing conference at City College, and—"

John interrupted him. "I don't think so, Chief. I took a course in writing one summer, but I'm not very good at it, and public speaking isn't—"

"What do you mean, you don't think so?" Chief barked. "This is not a *request*. It's an *order*."

"Oh," John said. "Now that you put it that way, I guess I'll be delighted."

"Besides," Chief said, "you don't know anything about crime solving, either, but you haven't let *that* stop you. You can talk a little about how to solve a crime and lead them through a mock mystery I've already set in motion. Then let the mystery writers try and solve it. If they're going to write about detective work, they'll need a little practice."

John hung up the phone and stumbled into the living room. "Rats! I was looking forward to relaxing today," he muttered as he gave Sebastian a friendly scratch between the ears.

Following John into the kitchen, Sebastian wriggled impatiently while his human opened a can of meat and dumped it into a bowl. He gobbled down its contents as John heated some water for instant coffee.

Sebastian licked the bowl sparkling clean and waited, hoping John would offer him a second helping. No luck.

He trotted into the bedroom behind John. He watched John sift through the clothes in his closet, then dress in a charcoal-colored houndstooth suit, muttering, "Why me?"

Sebastian couldn't see John's problem. After all, he would have his fuzzy partner to support him.

John grabbed his car keys from the dressing table, and Sebastian raced ahead of him toward the door. "Well, see you, old pal. Take care," John said, closing the door behind him.

Sebastian skidded to a halt so fast that the throw

rug wrinkled beneath him. See you? Take care? No way! He leaned his head back and howled at the top of his voice. *Aaarooooooooo! Oooooooooooooo!*

The door flung open. "No! Bad doggie. Lie down and be quiet," John commanded, then shut the door again.

That was not the proper response. Sebastian raised his voice an octave and tried again. *Aaarooooooooo! Oooooooooooooo!*

John pushed inside once more, his face ashen. "Don't *do* that!" he yelled. "You know the neighbors will complain."

Sebastian sat on his haunches and offered a paw to John.

"Oh, you know I can't resist that face," John said, laughing. "Come on."

Sebastian danced and spun, chasing his tail, then raced to the car. Actually, he was much too sophisticated for such things, but John expected this kind of behavior, and Sebastian hated to disappoint him.

Sebastian leaped into the passenger seat and looked out the window while John wove through the heavy traffic, muttering to himself. "What if I can't solve the mystery Chief set up? He's always looking for an excuse to fire me. This just might be it."

Sebastian reached over and kissed John on the

cheek to comfort him. He knew the power of a warm, wet puppy kiss.

John followed the signs to the parking lot nearest the Humanities Building, where the conference was taking place. He parked next to a battered blue Volkswagen Beetle.

Sebastian sprang from the car and trotted behind John up a short flight of stairs and into a hallway. There they encountered a group of animated people yelling at one another.

"My manuscript is missing from my briefcase," a woman said, "and I've got an appointment with the visiting editor this afternoon. I want it back right now!" She emphasized her demand with a stomp of her foot.

Did Sebastian and John have a *real* crime on their hands?

2
Crime on
Their Hands

When John had introduced himself, an older woman told him she was Keziah Autumn, president of the crime-writing club and organizer of the conference. "We were working on a mock mystery, but now Beatrice says her manuscript is missing. Isn't this exciting?"

Wearing a loose-fitting dress of gray challis trimmed with lace, Keziah Autumn looked more like Mother Goose than someone mixed up in crime, even fictional crime. She had purplish gray hair pushed into a knot on top of her head. Wisps as delicate as a spider's web escaped, and she continuously poked them back into the knot as she spoke.

John said, "If we go into the conference room, perhaps I can get to the bottom of this." He cupped his hands around his mouth and yelled, "Attention, everyone! Return to the conference room, please. Sit exactly where you were sitting before."

Still arguing and muttering among themselves, the group gradually returned to the room. Sebastian went in first and did a quick survey.

The conference room was a lecture hall with tiered rows of desks, a chalkboard up front, and a podium for the speaker. Several tables were placed at the front of the room. One held numerous implements of the criminal trade, everything from guns and knives to burglars' jimmies. Another held paper cups, milk, sugar, and a coffee urn. The third table held books and gold ballpoint pens, next to a sign that said TAKE ONE.

Sebastian sat near the door, studying the people as they entered. Which of them was the perpetrator?

The woman who had been yelling about a stolen manuscript was standing midway into the second row of seats. "That's my seat, Herbert! You agreed to trade with me so I could see the board better, remember." She wore long golden braids, a pinafore dress, and thick glasses, which she shoved up the bridge of her nose from time to time.

The object of her scolding was a shabbily dressed young man with hair like a lion's mane. The glare

16

he gave the woman would have frozen a lava flow, yet he gathered a stack of papers from the desk and traded seats without replying.

When everyone had been seated, John said, "I need to call my chief. Don't any of you move until I get back—please."

Sebastian was torn between the need to watch the room full of suspects and the need to satisfy his curiosity. Well, let the suspects watch one another. He followed John.

"Chief?" John said. "I'm sorry to phone you at home when you're not feeling well, but we have a little problem here. Somebody claims her manuscript has been stolen." Pausing, he shrugged. "Honest, Chief, I didn't do anything! Things were already a mess when I got here. Yes, sir, I understand: Solve it by tonight, or else."

John hung up, groaning. "I could've become anything, but, no, I wanted to be a cop. Why is life so complicated?"

Sebastian trotted back to the room with John. He touched his nose to John's hand to show his sympathy. But John didn't have to worry; the clever canine would solve the case and get him out of trouble with Chief.

Suddenly Sebastian's nose quivered. He inhaled

deeply, smelling chocolate doughnuts. He would help John later. After all, he had until evening—no problem.

Dashing into the room ahead of John, Sebastian spied a delectable platter full of doughnuts next to the coffeepot. *Ummmmmm,* nothing like chocolate in the morning to start the old crime-solving brain cells working.

Sebastian eased his way toward the table while John walked to the podium. "I have spoken with my boss, the chief of police, and he has assigned this case to me. As I understand it, you were working on a mock mystery that Chief set up for you, and in this game a manuscript was stolen? Whose?"

Keziah Autumn stepped up to the podium. She patted down her lace collar and smiled at John. "I was the absentminded professor who'd scribbled the formula to a new secret weapon on the back of her autobiography. My study was broken into, and the manuscript stolen."

Humph! Absentminded professor? What a cliché. Couldn't Chief think of a better mystery plot than that?

"Yes, ma'am," John said. "Now, which one of you was told to be the thief?"

"If the thief confesses, the game's over. We're

supposed to find out by investigating and detect-
ing," a man shouted from the audience.

"But, Rodger," Keziah said, "now we have a real
mystery to solve. Isn't that better?"

John sighed audibly. "As I was saying, which of
you is the pretend thief?"

A wizened hand slowly rose from the middle of
the room. An old man got to his feet. "I am the
clever, debonair double agent who double-crosses
both sides and takes the formula for himself, thereby
becoming a threat to world peace and a rich man."

Sebastian sank to the floor, covering his eyes with
his paws. That mystery scenario was so bad it hadn't
even been used for late-night cable movies.

"Never mind that silly mock mystery!" the woman
said. "I typed all night to have my manuscript ready
for my meeting this afternoon with the visiting
editor. I didn't even have enough time to have it
photocopied. It's my only copy. And, incidentally,
it's the best thing I've ever written."

The man called Herbert grabbed his throat as he
emitted a choking laugh. "That isn't saying a whole
lot," he muttered.

"And where was your manuscript the last time
you saw it?" John asked.

When Sebastian was sure that everyone's eyes

were directed toward the woman, he snatched a doughnut from the platter. Suddenly a jingling sound in the hall caught his attention, and he glanced toward the door, where a round face surrounded by carrot red hair peered inside. Violet-smeared eyelids fluttered as the woman's eyes flickered from Sebastian to the audience. Then she was gone.

Sebastian swallowed the doughnut in one gulp.

The writer of the missing manuscript stood up to answer John. "It was right here in my briefcase," she said.

"May I have your name, please," John said.

"I'm Beatrice Random. And my manuscript is called 'Dead Ahead,' about a murder at sea, and I want it back this instant!" She hit the desk with her gold ballpoint pen. Sniffling, she reached into her open handbag and pulled out a tissue. A second gold ballpoint pen with writing on it tumbled to the floor and rolled next to the dirty sneakers of the man with the lion's-mane hair.

The shaggy-haired man reached for the pen. Pausing only a second to gaze curiously at it, he handed it to Beatrice. She tossed the pen into her handbag without so much as a sidelong glance or a polite thank-you.

"It's pretty stupid to have only one copy of your manuscript," the man muttered in a voice loud enough for all of them to hear. "That's so amateur-ish."

Sebastian nodded his agreement. Beatrice had a backup pen, so why would she be so careless as to have only one copy of her manuscript?

"Well, I'm sorry, Herbert Henshaw, if I am not as professional as you mistakenly think you are. At least I've sold something."

Herbert glowered at Beatrice from beneath his knitted brows. He looked as if he were about to reply, but he didn't.

John cleared his throat. "There's an empty desk front and center. Is someone missing?"

Keziah laughed. "Oh, you can cross her off your suspect list. That seat belongs to our celebrity author, Violette Indigo. She's so successfully published that she doesn't need anything Beatrice would write." Keziah gasped. "No offense to your writing, Beatrice, dear. I just meant that Violette is so successful with her romantic suspense novels that she doesn't have to steal stories from anyone."

The expression on Keziah's face grew even more miserable when Herbert snorted loudly, but she continued, "She'll stroll in after lunch. She's a late sleeper."

"You mean she believes in grand entrances," Herbert said. "I saw her face at the door just a minute ago. I guess she didn't feel the time was right to come in."

Sebastian mulled over what he'd heard so far: The group had been playing a detective game about a stolen manuscript. And now there really was a stolen manuscript.

It appeared to be a case of copycat crime, and the ol' hairy hawkshaw had no less than a roomful of suspects, any one of them with a potential motive—jealousy, greed, revenge, or a host of others.

Suddenly, tonight seemed too early a deadline for solving the crime.

3

No Crime Like the Present

John checked his watch. "Well, we're running way behind the schedule. It's already time for the lunch break. I want all of you to leave your belongings, except for your wallets and handbags, in this room. Nothing is to be taken out until we have gotten to the bottom of this."

Herbert shifted in his chair. "You don't have any right to do that!"

Sebastian curled his lip and emitted a low growl of disapproval.

"Unless I discover otherwise," John said, "I am assuming that a genuine crime has taken place, and, exercising my authority as a police official, I declare this a crime scene. We can stay here while I investigate—and miss lunch, incidentally—or you can cooperate with me, and we can eat."

Sebastian's chest nearly burst with pride. His human was handling this case just as he, Sebastian (Super Sleuth), would.

"Yeah, Herbert," Beatrice said, "cooperate. Unless you took my manuscript, that is."

"Get real, Bea," Herbert growled. "You don't write anything worth stealing. Maybe you didn't have a manuscript at all. Maybe you're just saying that to save face with the editor."

Keziah tapped the table. "People, people, we are here to help one another, not to snipe. I say we do exactly as Detective Jones says. But I issue a challenge. Let's see who can solve this mystery first, one of us or Detective Jones."

The crowd burst into applause. "Yes!" someone shouted. "A duel of detectives!"

Oh, his poor human. Now John not only had to solve the mystery by nightfall, but he also had to solve it before one of these amateur detectives did. What if one of them solved it first? How embarrassing. If only John knew that his fuzzy buddy would never let a thing like that happen— Sebastian hoped.

Sebastian stood with John by the door while the writers filed through, one at a time.

Keziah and Herbert were the last to leave. She spoke briefly with Herbert. "I think the conference would be more harmonious if you and I traded seats, Herbert. You and Beatrice shouldn't be anywhere near each other."

Keziah put her papers on Herbert's desk, and he moved to her desk near the door. When they had left, John shut the door. He reached into his pocket and pulled out a roll of crime-scene tape and stretched a measure of it across the door and doorjamb. The tape would be easily torn if anyone opened the door.

Catching up with Keziah, John asked her, "Is there a place where I can stow my dog while we eat and then for the afternoon? He'll just be in the way of the investigation."

Sebastian came to a screeching halt. Why, without this four-on-the-floor detective, there'd be no investigation worth speaking of. Besides, the cafeteria was the perfect place to take him.

"The mascot is away with the football team," Keziah said. "You ought to be able to use his kennel. I'll ask the dean's office." She made a phone call, and soon the reluctant canine was being dragged, kicking and whimpering, to a small kennel near the campus reflecting pool, where he was shut in like a common criminal—or worse, like an ordinary dog.

When John turned to leave, Sebastian threw back his head and let out a resounding *Aaarooooooooo-oooooooooooooooo!*

"That's not going to work this time, pal," John called over his shoulder. "See you later."

There was no point in looking hangdog or playing any of the usual tricks. John didn't even look back.

Sighing miserably, Sebastian decided there was only one thing to do. He got as far back in the kennel run as he could, then made a romping dash toward the gate. Springing at the last moment, he clung to the fence with his front paws and kicked feverishly until he managed to tug the rest of himself over the top. There wasn't a fence anywhere that could hold this Houdini hound!

Now for a disguise. He needed something that would admit him into the cafeteria now and into the conference later. But what?

Sebastian raced along the path and scooted into the Humanities Building behind a student, who was distracted as she juggled textbooks and the door.

He trotted down the hall, looking into open door-ways. A sports letter jacket—no. A raincoat—no.

27

Ah! A tweed jacket with elbow patches and a fedora—now, that says mystery writer!

With just a wriggle and a twist, the costumed canine emerged into the hall, blending in with the humanities students who were milling around, chatting. He scampered out the door behind a swoop of students and followed them to the cafeteria.

Shoving his tray along the counter, he paused to let the servers fill his plate with a hot helping of potatoes and gravy, a succulent slice of braised sirloin, and a pile of purple peas.

"That'll be three dollars and twenty cents, sir," the cashier said.

Uh-oh! Sebastian had forgotten that humans expected to be paid for food. Now what?

"Oh, brother," the cashier said. "You professors, always conveniently forgetting to bring your wallets." She shoved the receipt toward him. "Sign it as an IOU, and you can pay later," she said, laughing.

"That's okay," a young woman said. "I'll get it. Just remember this when I get you for a class, sir."

Sebastian nodded his thanks and hurried with his tray to where he saw the writers gathered. He took an empty chair across from Keziah and Beatrice and

next to Herbert. Keeping his head down and his ears alert, he eavesdropped.

The woman who had been identified earlier as Violette Indigo was seated at one end of the table, nibbling on a piece of fried chicken and explaining to the group where she got the ideas for her stories. "I read the newspapers and watch the news and keep my eyes and ears open for the smallest morsel of interesting information. Then I just let my vivid imagination take over," she said. "And my writing skills, of course." Her charm bracelet jingled as she waved her hands about.

All heads at the table bobbed in agreement—all except Herbert's. He muttered into his salad.

Violette glanced briefly at Herbert. "Well, umm, yes, we can't all be successful, I suppose. But we must keep trying, mustn't we?" She pushed her chair back. "If you'll excuse me, I believe I'll freshen up before the next session."

Beatrice leaned across the table until she was eye to eye with Herbert. "You are the most negative person I know, putting everybody down. Besides, if my writing is so lousy, how come I have sold a short story to *The Future Is Ours* magazine?"

"Because despite your antiquated writing style, the editors liked the idea, which was mine in the first place," Herbert mumbled before taking another bite of tofu salad.

"That's it!" Beatrice said. "I'm not going to sit here and let you insult me." She grabbed her tray and stalked from the cafeteria.

"Oh, dear," Keziah said. "Why do you provoke her like that, Herbert, especially when she's already upset? I had better go find her and apologize."

"Don't apologize for me!" Herbert said, snorting. "I said the truth. The only good idea she's had is the one she stole from me. I'm tired of people getting credit for my work." Herbert stood up so fast that his chair fell back. He stalked out of the cafeteria without replacing the chair or taking his tray.

Keziah excused herself, shaking her head sadly. "Incidents like this can spoil a conference for everyone," she moaned as she hastily left through the side door.

There was no need to let food go to waste. Sebastian rolled his tongue across the salad. *Blah!* Tofu was yucky. It tasted like wet cement. No wonder Herbert was grouchy.

With Keziah, Beatrice, Herbert, and Violette gone, the rest of the conference group settled into a quiet lunch. Before long there was a general scraping of chairs as the members took their trays back to the collection window and left the cafeteria. Sebastian fell into step at the rear of the group.

When they all reached the conference room, someone shrieked, and John yelled, "What is this?"

The curious canine wriggled his way to the front of the group. Then he saw what had caused the disturbance.

The crime scene tape was broken. Someone had been in the room during their absence.

4
Crime after Crime

"Everyone, take your seats and check your belongings," John instructed the writers. Sebastian found an empty chair where he could observe everyone.

Keziah approached Sebastian. "Oh, our late conferee! Welcome to the group." She pinned to his jacket a badge that said Wayne Nuggat.

Sebastian nodded gratefully.

Feet were scraped and papers shuffled, and voices muttered displeasure. Then Keziah Autumn gasped. "Oh, no! Now *my* manuscript is gone, my *children's* story."

John held up his hand to silence the raised voices. "I must remind everyone that crossing a crime-scene barrier is prosecutable. However, if this is some sort of joke, the prankster may return the missing manuscripts, and we can just forget this ever happened."

The door opened, and Violette Indigo, with a jingling of jewelry and a look of exasperation on her face, rushed into the room. She stood a moment scowling at John, then at the conferees, as she nervously patted her hair into place. She took a deep breath, squared her shoulders, and smoothed her dress. She smiled at everyone. "Sorry, my dears. Am I late?"

For a woman who had left the group to "freshen up," Violette looked woefully disheveled to Sebastian. She must have run all the way, and she might even have fallen since there were traces of green along the sides of her dress. Grass stains? Sebastian wondered.

John motioned for her to sit down. "We were just beginning our investigation of the missing manuscripts," he explained.

She fluttered her purple-lidded eyes at John. "Oh, of course, the little game we're playing."

"It's no game, Violette," Beatrice said. "First my manuscript was stolen, and now Keziah's. And it's for real."

Violette shook her head sadly. "Oh, dear, what a

shame. I will certainly keep an eye on my manuscript."

The conferees looked at one another, then at John, but no one came forth with the manuscripts.

Shrugging, John said, "If I remember from the creative writing class I took many years ago, we detectives ask basically the same questions that you writers ask. As writers, you get to make up the answers. We detectives, however, must find the truth. So let's start with the questions. Anyone?"

Hands shot up all around the room, and the questions pelted the air like popping corn.

"Who?"

"What?"

"When?"

"Where?"

"Why?"

"How?"

Sebastian's ears flapped as he turned first toward one voice, then toward another.

"Right," John said, nodding and smiling. "*Who* is the perpetrator? *What* did he or she take? *When* was it last seen? *Where* was it when it was stolen? *Why* did he or she steal it? And *how* has the perp succeeded—so far?"

Cheers and whistles erupted, and Sebastian broke

into a panting grin. These amateurs had all the right questions. But it would be up to the experts to find the correct answers.

John turned toward the chalkboard. He wrote the capital letters M.O.M. "To find the answers to those questions, we must look for M.O.M. Not Mom, as in Mother, but M period, O period, M period. Motive, opportunity, and means."

While all the heads were bobbing yes, John continued. "Motives are as varied as people. Think about why anyone would want to steal a manuscript." John looked the group over. "Any ideas?"

Beatrice raised her hand. "I know! I know! Jealousy. I vote for Herbert."

"But, Bea, dear," Keziah said, "I haven't sold anything. So why would he steal mine?"

"Er," John said, "we can't elect a criminal, ma'am. We have to follow the clues to reach the solution. And there are plenty of motives beyond jealousy—greed, revenge, and anger, to name a few."

And ambition, Sebastian mentally added. His mouth split into a panting grin.

John continued. "Some suspects may have a motive. Perhaps they also had the *opportunity* to commit the crime. That is, they were in the vicinity of the crime. Or perhaps they can't account for their

time or whereabouts, so they *appear* to have had the opportunity."

Sebastian couldn't speak for the first manuscript, but he knew of four people—Beatrice, Herbert, Violette, and Keziah—who had left the cafeteria early, in time to take the second one. Keziah, of course, wouldn't steal her own manuscript—unless she had taken the first one and wanted to throw suspicion off herself by pretending her own manuscript had been stolen. Could all of these people account for their time?

John said, "The remaining test is means, the skill or know-how to commit the crime. Everyone here passes that one, so it won't be of much help in narrowing our list of suspects. One or more people will pass all three tests—they'll have motive, opportunity, and means, or M.O.M. This is where witnesses come in. Sometimes they can dispute the suspects' stories.

"And the crime scene itself provides good clues. Every thief may take something away, but he also leaves something behind—a print, a single hair, lint from his clothes, or any number of clues," John said. "It's up to the detective to discover what it is that the thief has left at the crime scene. There you

38

have it. Why don't you folks ponder these questions a bit while I conduct my investigation."

Sebastian admired how simply John had described their job. It was a shame that his human was more of a theory man than a man of action. John was lucky to have the hairy hawkshaw!

The classroom door squeaked on its hinges as Herbert Henshaw came in and glumly slid into his chair. "Sorry I'm late," he mumbled. "I found my car had a flat tire and I had to change it."

"We ought to check for fingerprints," Beatrice said.

John shook his head. "Folks put too much faith in fingerprints. They work only when a surface has been freshly cleaned or painted and doesn't have many layers of prints. Just imagine the last time that classroom door was thoroughly cleaned."

"Euu," Keziah said. "Speaking of fingerprints, look at my hand. The gold on that giveaway pen is turning my fingers green, and now I've smudged my notes."

Beatrice snickered. "It isn't gold, silly. You think Violette's publisher would use real gold for giveaways? These are copies of the gold one they gave her when her first suspense sold a million copies."

Beatrice examined her own fingers. "Hmm, mine's not doing that."

Sebastian strained to see. Sure enough, Keziah's fingers were tipped in a tarnished green. Was it tarnish and not grass stains on Violette's dress? Maybe the publisher had given her a phony gold pen, too.

John wiggled a finger at Beatrice. "Why don't I talk with you first. When did you discover that your manuscript was missing?"

Beatrice shoved her heavy glasses back up on the bridge of her nose and fluffed the straps of her pinafore before leaping to her feet. "The room was open when I got here this morning, and the coffee in the urn was still perking. I put my briefcase right here, so I could see the board better than I could yesterday. I put my handbag on the floor, sort of out of sight, removed my billfold, and went to the cafeteria for coffee. Then I walked around the campus a bit. When I returned, there was still no one in here, but my manuscript was gone."

Sebastian edged closer so that he could catch every word. What time had all this taken place?

"And what time did you leave and return to the room?" John asked Beatrice.

Beatrice said, "I got here around nine and left

soon after. I returned around thirty minutes later."

"It was Herbert's turn to make the coffee!" Rodger yelled from the back of the room.

Herbert turned in his seat to glare. "So what, Rodger?"

John was jotting on paper what the old hairy hawkshaw was committing to memory. Next John called on Keziah. "You say that your manuscript was on your desk at noon when I sealed the room with the crime-scene tape?"

Keziah tucked the silky strands of her hair back into the knot. "Yes, I'm quite sure. I would've noticed if anything was gone when I changed desks."

Sebastian wriggled with pent-up energy. What was the common thread between the two manuscripts? Beatrice's manuscript was a full-length adult mystery about a murder at sea, and Keziah's was a children's story.

Sebastian reviewed the clues. Herbert had made the coffee that morning, so he may have been in the room after Beatrice left her manuscript. He and Beatrice were bickering constantly. He and Keziah weren't what you'd call friends, either. In fact, Herbert seemed to be on the outs with everyone at the conference.

But why would Herbert take the manuscripts? And what did he do with them? And how was the old super sleuth going to prove it before the evening deadline?

"Dah-lings," Violette said, "all of this is quite upsetting to my delicate system. It has given me a splitting headache. If I may be excused, I'll retire to my dorm room and take some aspirin."

Keziah reached into her purse. "I have some right here, Violette."

Sputtering, Violette thanked Keziah. "But I really must use my own. Delicate system, you understand."

"Then meet us at the reflecting pool," Keziah said, "if that's all right with Detective Jones. We're supposed to have a tea break there in about ten minutes."

Teatime already? Sebastian glanced at the big round clock at the front of the room. It was already three o'clock. Didn't time fly when he had a deadline?

5
Crime Waits for No One

John had no objections, so the group moved like a gaggle of geese toward the reflecting pool. It was located in the center of a cluster of imposing buildings.

To one side was a building about toolshed size. Curious, Sebastian rose on his hind legs and peered through the window. He saw a huge, greasy pipe with something like a steering wheel on it. Water stood about ankle deep on the floor. This was clearly the pump room, with the controls for purifying and filling the pool.

When Sebastian rejoined the conferees, they were having cups of tea and brownie squares. He skipped the tea and snatched a couple of brownie squares, gulping them with appreciation.

"Have you been published yet?" Beatrice asked Sebastian.

He growled softly.

"I understand your feelings completely, but don't take that attitude with me!" She turned away.

Milling around to listen to the conversations, he heard Beatrice talking with Rodger. "Violette has certainly been successful selling her books. Sometimes I wonder why she is and the rest of us aren't. Even Herbert writes well enough to publish, but you better never tell him I said so."

Rodger leaned forward and whispered so softly that the keen-eared canine had difficulty hearing. "I've heard rumors that she didn't really write all those books, that she hired a ghostwriter. I'd never want to ghostwrite; I want to see my name in big letters on the cover."

Sebastian meandered toward another group. "Herbert's attitude is probably what keeps him from publishing," Keziah was telling several of the writers. "He's published in some of those literary magazines that don't pay, and he attended college here on a writing scholarship."

"No, he didn't!" a woman said. "I work in the registrar's office, and I'm positive he paid cash for all four years." She flushed. "I—I was curious about him and pulled his records."

Keziah tucked some flyaway wisps of hair into her

bun. "How curious! Why would he have told us he'd had a four-year scholarship?"

Sebastian agreed. Herbert was a real puzzle. And a real suspect in the theft of Beatrice's manuscript. He had motive: revenge, because he really believed she'd stolen his idea, or maybe even a plan to ask for ransom, since Beatrice had no other copies. He'd had opportunity: early arrival to make the coffee and an unguarded manuscript, which he could have taken when he returned. And he had means: He'd have had plenty of time to dispose of or hide the manuscript.

And what about Keziah's manuscript? Had it been taken just to throw the cunning canine off the trail? Was it a red herring?

Beatrice had eased her way to where Herbert and Keziah were standing near the edge of the pool, watching the goldfish cavort. Sebastian followed.

Violette, who had joined them at poolside, pointed skyward. "Oh, look! What kind of lovely bird is that?"

Suddenly Beatrice shrieked as she plunged into the pool. "I can't swim! Help! I'll drown!"

Without thinking of his own safety, the heroic hawkshaw leaped into the pool. He'd save her!

Sebastian had almost reached her when Herbert

gave a roaring laugh. "Stand up, dummy! It's only three feet deep!" He reached for Beatrice's hand to pull her up, and she yanked hard, pulling him in, too. The other conferees laughed and applauded.

Sebastian dog-paddled to the side of the pool and pulled himself onto the bank. He shook hard, sending water spraying in every direction, then rolled in the grass to squeeze water out of his jacket. The fedora drooped, almost obscuring his view.

The other conferees were focused on John as he helped Beatrice and Herbert out of the pool.

"My goodness, how did you two fall in?" he asked.

"I did not fall in!" Beatrice snarled as she wrung out the hem of her pinafore. She plucked a lily pad off her shoulder and tossed it back into the pool. "Herbert pushed me in!"

6
One at a Crime, Please

John scratched his head. "Are you sure you were pushed? Are you positive it was Herbert who pushed you?" John asked Beatrice.

Beatrice shook her head no and her water-soaked pigtails slung water. "No, not exactly. I was looking for the bird Violette was talking about. But who else could it have been?"

Almost any one of the conferees, Sebastian recalled. They were all huddled together and looking skyward. If only he'd kept his eyes on the crowd. An avid bird-watcher always hoping to spot a rare one, he'd allowed himself to be momentarily distracted.

"Whoever pushed me did it deliberately. I felt two strong hands against my back, and everyone in the group *knows* that I can't swim. Everyone except him!" Beatrice said, shivering. She pointed at Sebastian. "I've got a change of clothes in my car. Excuse me."

Most of the group returned to the conference room. Herbert, who had gotten as wet as Sebastian and Beatrice, was missing, and so was Violette. Perhaps she'd gotten splattered.

The voices of the conferees sounded like the buzzing of a fluorescent light gone bad.

"I think I smell a wet dog!" Rodger said.

Sebastian slumped farther down in his chair. It must be the poor blend of wool in this jacket, he thought.

Moments later, Beatrice returned in a pair of gray slacks and a matching sweatshirt. She was wearing running shoes instead of the sandals she'd had on earlier.

"Does anyone know the whereabouts of Herbert and Violette?" John asked.

The door burst open and Violette swept in. Even though she squared her shoulders and held her head at an appropriately dignified angle, her entrance was something less than queenly. Her right sleeve had a dark smudge on it, and her shoes squished as she walked, leaving a distinct trail of wet prints. At least she wasn't jingling. She'd taken

off her charm bracelet. She plopped into her chair, breathing heavily.

John let a long sigh escape. "We're still missing Herbert."

"He said he was going home to change clothes," Violette said. "Perhaps I should put his things somewhere safe."

Beatrice glanced out the window. "That old Volkswagen is Herbert's. Maybe he changed his mind."

Scowling, John nodded toward Sebastian. "Sir, would you hand me that backpack and notebook? I'll see that it gets back to him."

Sebastian snatched the backpack, using the opportunity to glance at its contents. How odd! Inside Herbert's backpack were tennis shoes, shorts, and a T-shirt. Why would he have gone home to change if he had clothes with him? And how would he have gone home if his car was still in the parking lot? The four-on-the-floor furry detective had a feeling that something was definitely wrong.

7
Crime for a Solution

Two manuscripts had been stolen, and Beatrice had been pushed into the pool by unseen hands. Herbert, the least likely hero of the day, had offered her a helping hand and had gotten dunked for his trouble. Now he was missing.

Violette, who had straggled in sloshing and smudged, had said Herbert was going home to change clothes. Yet his car was still in the parking lot and his backpack contained a change of clothes. Why had he told Violette that he was going to get some clothes? Or had he?

But why would she lie? And why was she so

disheveled? What were those smudges, anyway?

Sebastian dropped his pen so that he had an excuse to bend over. In that position, he was able to sniff the smudge on Violette's dress. Grease. Now where would she pick up a grease stain? And why were her shoes all wet when there was not a splatter of water on her dress?

As he rose back up, Sebastian knocked over Beatrice's handbag, and out tumbled two pens. One was a shiny gold, and the other was clearly one of the giveaways.

How did Beatrice wind up with Violette's real pen? Sebastian remembered that earlier Violette had smeared her dress with gold tarnish. Why didn't she mention that her real gold pen was missing?

All of this had to be connected in some way, and Herbert was no doubt in the middle of it. But how? And why?

It seemed that crime followed Herbert around the room. He'd traded seats with Beatrice, and her manuscript had been stolen. Then he'd traded seats with Keziah, and *her* manuscript had been stolen. And he'd been standing beside Beatrice when she was knocked into the pool.

What if these women weren't the target? What if someone had intended to steal *Herbert's* manuscript and hadn't realized that he and Beatrice, and then he and Keziah, had traded seats? That had to be it! But why? And who wouldn't know about the trades?

Then it hit Sebastian. The only conferee who had not been around when the exchanges were made was Violette. But why was she trying to get Herbert?

The pen! Herbert had examined it briefly when Beatrice had dropped it. He must have noticed then that it was real gold and therefore Violette's, yet he hadn't said anything. Why hadn't he spoken up?

Sebastian suddenly remembered where he'd smelled something like that smudge before—on John's lawnmower. It was machine oil. But where had Violette been with machines?

His tail wagged enthusiastically as the answer came to him. Sebastian leaped from his chair and pushed open the door, dashing down the hall and shedding clothes as he went. He raced toward the pool, where Herbert had last been seen.

At the shed, Sebastian rose on his hind legs, peering through the dust- and grease-smudged window.

Yes, he was there! Herbert was neatly tied to the pool's pump handle. Sebastian raced around to the door, scratching furiously.

John came up, panting, and it seemed that the entire class had followed him. "Sebastian, I thought I saw you out here! Bad doggie! You escaped from the kennel. Shame! Come, now."

Sebastian ignored John and continued to scratch on the door, whimpering and whining.

Keziah said, "When my dog scratches on the door, it's because he wants out. I think your dog is trying to tell us something."

"No," John said. "He's just trying to hide from me because he knows he's been a bad dog, getting out of the kennel like that."

Keziah cocked her head and said, "I think I hear muffled noises in there."

"And I think we should go back to the conference room," Violette said. "We're getting behind schedule, and it'll soon be time to autograph books. The newspaper reporter and photographer will be here in a little while."

Keziah jerked on the door. "It's not locked."

"It says No Admittance," Violette said.

Keziah turned the knob and pushed open the

door. "Herbert!" she yelled. "Look, it's Herbert, and he's gagged and tied up."

John sloshed through the standing water and knelt to untie Herbert. "Who did this to you?" he asked.

"I didn't see," Herbert said, rubbing his wrists. "Someone hit me from behind, and when I woke up, I was bound." He glared into the crowd of onlookers who stood outside the shed, peering in curiously. "I have a pretty good idea, though."

"Well, that wouldn't be good enough to bring charges against anyone," John said, pulling at his sleeve. "Oh, rats. An oil smudge on my good suit; I wonder if that will come out. And my shoes!" John wailed. "They're soaked."

John was almost there! He had all the clues he needed: smudged clothes, wet shoes. Would he get it?

"Well," John said, "I suppose we'd better return to the conference room and try to puzzle this thing out."

Frantically, Sebastian tried to push John to look at the clues, but he couldn't get him to notice. Then he had an idea. Keziah! If he couldn't make John understand, maybe he could make Keziah understand. Sebastian scampered around the group, yipping in his best imitation of a puppy out of control. Then he quickly swung his rump into Violette, shoving her toward Keziah.

"Oh!" Keziah said. "Sor—" She swept her purplish gray hair from her eyes and stared, open-mouthed. "Violette, look at you! Oh, Detective Jones! Look! Look at Violette's dress. Look at her shoes! She has a smudge on her sleeve, just like you do. And she has wet shoes but she hasn't been inside the pump house, I recall."

Just then, Sebastian saw something shiny in the water by the pump handle. It was Violette's charm bracelet. He sloshed into the water and pawed at it, whimpering.

At first John scolded Sebastian for getting in the water; then he noticed the bracelet, too. "Hmm," John said. "I think we should return to the conference room. It's time to wrap up this case."

As the story unfolded, Herbert, who seemed to pride himself on being so literary, admitted that he had paid for his college education by ghostwriting Stormie Wethers stories for Violette. She had run out of ideas, yet the series was too popular to give up. He'd answered an anonymous ad in a magazine and had sent all of his material to a postal box, so they hadn't met until she'd come to speak at this conference.

Violette had promised to share her royalties with Herbert, but she had not. At the time of their meeting, Herbert refused to give her the next manuscript until she honored her promise. Since her editor was reminding her of her deadline, Violette threatened to expose his ghostwriting to the press. This would no doubt be an embarrassment to him.

"I knew she didn't want her own deception revealed to her public," Herbert said, "but I wasn't anxious to have people know I'd been writing those sappy heroine stories, either."

Beatrice burst out laughing. "Herbert the Horrible, author of Stormie Wethers stories! What a hoot!"

Herbert snarled at Beatrice, then continued. "Then Beatrice's manuscript was stolen. When I noticed Violette's pen in Beatrice's purse, I figured that Violette had accidentally dropped it as she'd grabbed the manuscript, which she thought was mine."

Of course, the clever canine agreed. And when

the second manuscript was stolen from where Herbert had been sitting *before* he switched seats with Beatrice, that was even more proof. He had been in his previous seat when Violette had peeked inside.

"I just wanted to hold his manuscript until he promised not to tell my editor," Violette said. "I didn't mean any harm. Keziah, Beatrice, your manuscripts are in my dorm room." She dabbed at her eyes. "I really am sorry."

"Why did you knock me into the water?" Beatrice demanded.

"I didn't mean to. I was aiming at Herbert and missed. I just wanted a reason for him not to return to the conference room. I wanted a chance to talk to him, to convince him to keep writing for Stormie Wethers." She smiled. "But then you helped me, Beatrice, dear, by pulling him into the water, so it worked out just fine, anyway."

"It might have," John said, "if it hadn't been for my ridiculous dog romping around loose."

Deep in his throat, Sebastian rumbled indignantly. John gave him no credit at all!

With the case cleared up and the manuscripts returned, the writers gave John a round of applause for solving the mystery.

Keziah walked with John and Sebastian to the parking lot. "I have this story idea about a dog detective who thinks like people," she told John. "What would you say to something like 'Petunia, Private Eye,' or maybe 'Clover, K-9 Cop'?"

Sebastian pulled back his fuzzy lips in a big smile. What a wonderful idea! But what was wrong with "Sebastian (Super Sleuth)"?

"Oh, ma'am," John said, laughing, "dogs can't think like people. And how would they investigate without our noticing them? Sorry, ma'am, it just wouldn't work."

Sebastian broke into a panting grin. Did John have a lot to learn!